Princess Of Feathers

Grimm Academy #16

Laura Greenwood

CONTENTS

BLURB

Elisa has always known about her deadly prophecy, but the last thing she expected was for the swans to arrive in the form of her cursed brothers.

With her friends desperate for her to take part in the Princess Competition, and her new courtship taking a turn towards serious, Elisa already has her hands full. And when she discovers her chances of getting out of her prophecy alive hinges on a vow of silence, things become even more complicated.

Can Elisa save her brothers in time?

Princess Of Feathers is a fantasy academy romance inspired by The Wild Swans fairy tale. It includes a sweet m/f romance. It is part of the Grimm Academy series.

PROLOGUE

A small crowd of students gather outside the dining hall of Grimm Academy. I frown, wondering what they're doing there.

I turn to Astrid, half expecting her to have the answer. She always seems to know what's going on, though I have no idea where she's getting her information. Maybe the furniture is whispering to her. It wouldn't be the first time something strange has happened here, especially amongst the students who have prophecies about them. Myself included.

A shiver runs down my spine at the thought of it. Most of the time, I just pretend it's not a big deal, but I don't think that'll last much longer.

Astrid simply shrugs. "Don't look at me, I have no idea what's going on."

I sigh. The *one* time she doesn't know is when it looks interesting. That's just typical.

"Mati said something about a competition," Cordelia puts in.

I raise an eyebrow. I don't know her older sister very well, mostly Matilda keeps to herself. I think she still blames herself for getting Cordelia banished from their home alongside her.

"For what?" Astrid asks.

"Something about Bellpoint Castle. I wasn't really listening."

I gasp. "Bellpoint? Are you sure that's right?"

"I think that's what she said. Why, what is it?" She tips her head to the side.

"And why is it stopping us getting to lunch?" Astrid mutters.

"You haven't heard of the Bellpoint competition?" I ask, glancing between my two friends.

"Should we have?" Astrid asks pointedly.

Hmm. I suppose not. Astrid is the daughter of a wealthy merchant, but hasn't been around nobility much until she came to the academy, and Cordelia has spent most of her life under the sea and away from humans.

"Bellpoint Castle and the surrounding kingdom don't use succession law to pick their heir. The reigning King or Queen calls for a competition when they're ready to appoint an heir. People between the ages of seventeen and twenty throughout the kingdoms can compete, and if they win, they're crowned the heir," I explain.

"And they become a princess?" Astrid whispers.

I nod. I know it bothers that she's the only one of the three of us without a title, even if neither Cordelia or I will ever have a kingdom. Not with my three older brothers and her being estranged from her family. Even if she wasn't, she's younger than her other siblings too.

"Who can compete?" Cordelia asks.

"Anyone."

"So we could sign up?" Excitement comes through Astrid's question.

"Yes, if we wanted." I shrug.

"We should do it."

My gaze flicks to Cordelia, not having expected her to be the one to suggest something like that.

"It would be nice not to rely on Mati and her fiancé for the rest of my life."

Ah. That does make sense. I hadn't thought about it like that, but I can see why she wants to win.

"And it's not like either of you have a kingdom to run either," she continues. "We should all do it."

"I don't need..." I start.

"You're doing it," Astrid responds, reaching out and grabbing my hand.

"It would be better if one of you won," I point out. I don't need a kingdom. My older brothers would all make sure I'm taken care of.

"But if we're all part of the competition, then we can help each other," Astrid points out. "And that way, even if you don't win, you can help one of us do it instead."

"Fine. I'll do it," I agree. "But only so I can help you both."

That's all the encouragement the two of them need and they drag me through the assembled student to the wall where the sign-up sheet is.

Astrid goes first, leaving the two of us standing behind her and waiting nervously while she signs. Once she's done, she passes the pencil to Cordelia who adds her name and details to the sheet.

A small part of me wants to go against Astrid and not sign up. I don't need this, and I don't want to take the opportunity away from the people who deserve it more. Or even those who desire it more than I do. This isn't something I've ever needed.

But it is a once in a lifetime opportunity. Or even rarer than that. Two of my brothers aren't able to take part due to their age.

"Elisa? Are you all right?" Cordelia asks.

"Hmm? Sorry. I was distracted."

"I guessed that when you didn't take the pencil. But you should hurry up and sign up before anyone starts getting annoyed at you.

I nod and take it from her.

The list is already dozens of names long. It seems like everyone of the right age at the academy has signed up, which isn't much of a surprise. There are plenty of people who study here who would benefit from becoming the heir to a kingdom, even a small one like Bellpoint.

I don't waste any more time and lean in to write my name. I'm still not sure about taking part, but I want to help my friends and this is the best way I can do that. Without being part of the competition, I won't have any way of being able to keep up with what's going on. I've heard they don't tell outsiders what each of the tasks is going to be.

"Done." I hand the pencil to the next person in line and turn to my friends.

"Good. Now, let's go to lunch." Astrid loops one of her arms through mine and does the same with Cordelia. The three of us make our way into the dining room.

I accidentally bump into someone as we make our way past.

"Sorry," I say quickly.

"It was my fault," the boy in front of me counters. "I'm sorry too."

"Are you all right? I didn't hurt you?"

Astrid slips her arm out of mine and disappears to get some food with Cordelia.

"I'm fine. Are you?" he asks.

I nod quickly.

"I don't think we've met," he says.

"No. Are you new here?"

"More or less. What's your name?"

"Elisa. Yours?"

"Alaric."

It suits him. I'm not sure why, but he looks like an Alaric. I don't know whether it's the auburn slightly curly hair, or the shoulders that suggest he'll grow into a strong frame.

A furious blush rises to my cheeks as I realise I'm standing there staring at him.

"It's nice to meet you," I mumble.

"You too, Elisa, I hope to see you around." A genuine smile lights up his face.

"I'm sure you will."

"Your friends are waiting for you." He nods in the direction of Cordelia and Astrid, who are try-ing their best not to be caught watching.

"They probably just want to know who you are." And will want a full rundown of the entire con-versation, even if it isn't going to be a particularly thrilling reveal.

Alaric chuckles. "Good luck."

"Thanks. I'll see you in class." I wave and head over to where my friends are already giggling and waiting for me to return to them.

I hope they got me some food.

CHAPTER 1

Our dancing teacher taps the ground, demanding the attention of everyone in the room. I hate it when he does that, the sound goes right through me.

"Get into positions, everyone," he calls. "There are some new members of the class, so please be ready to teach them the steps."

"Isn't that what he's supposed to do?" Astrid mutters beside me.

I let out a small laugh. "I think it's several years too late for that."

"True. I'm just grateful you were here when I moved up to this class, I'd never have managed to catch up with what I'm supposed to know."

"Hmm. Maybe."

The teacher raps on the floor again, stopping our conversation mid-flow.

"Let the dance begin," he announces, gesturing to the musicians in the corner.

The first notes of the song wash through the room, sending us all into action. I curtsy to the man in front of me.

He bows in return and holds out a hand. I take it and we start going through the motions of the dance. I don't recognise him, which doesn't mean much. He seems to be concentrating on the steps, but is doing them close to perfectly, so I don't say anything.

Astrid stumbles in front of me, but rights herself quickly enough. She has so much natural grace, but she struggles with some of the more rigid aspects of the dance.

I let go of my dance partner's hand and walk out in a semi-circle as part of the dance. By the time I return to my spot, he's been replaced by a familiar face.

"It's been a while," Alaric says, a genuine smile spreading over his face.

"I didn't realise you'd be joining our dance class."

"Neither did I, it was a surprise when I arrived this morning. But I have to say, the company is delightful."

My heart flutters at the compliment even if it's typical courtroom flirting.

"Do you know the steps?" I ask.

"More or less. But I feel like I need some one-on-one tuition." He grins as if he knows exactly what he's suggesting. I can't say I'm opposed to the idea.

"I can help. I've been dancing since I was old enough to walk."

"It shows."

"The advantage of being the doted on only girl. My father made sure I had lessons in all of the arts of being the perfect princess."

"I didn't realise you were one," he says as we come closer together thanks to the come and go of the dance.

"The advantage of no one using titles here."

"You don't like being a princess?"

I spin under his arm. "It's fine, but I don't like it defining who I am."

"That's fair. But it's made you a beautiful dancer."

"Thank you." A small blush steals over my face. "You're not bad yourself."

He chuckles. "Mother thought it would help me attract the kind of girl who would increase the prestige of our family name."

I raise an eyebrow. "Does that work?"

"You tell me. Have you ever been attracted to someone because of how good of a dancer they are?" While part of his question seems to be in jest, there's also a serious note to it.

I spin under his arm while contemplating what my answer actually is.

"I suppose I've not *not* been attracted to someone because they're a good dancer."

Alaric laughs, drawing the attention of the dancing teacher. He glares at us, but turns away as soon as he realises we're doing a good job of his choreography.

"I see the point. If someone is a particularly bad dancer, it'll probably put me off spending time with them at balls, so I won't get to know them as well as I otherwise could. But I'd much rather have someone who felt like they could talk to me than someone who would only ever dance."

"Why do I feel like I have to congratulate you on your answer?" he asks.

I let a small smile lift the corners of my lips. "Because you do. It was a good one."

"It was," he agrees. "I think it might even deserve a celebratory dinner in the village, if you would be open to that."

"I would," I say without thinking twice about it.

A wide grin spreads over Alaric's face. "I'll meet you in the entrance hall after class?"

"You want to go tonight?"

"Maybe I don't want to give you a chance to change your mind."

"That wouldn't be very nice of you," I point out.

"You're right, it wouldn't be. Really I just don't want to wait to get to know you better."

"Much better answer," I assure him.

The music comes to an end and the two of us part. I dip into a deep curtsy just as he bows. I'm not sure what causes it, but something feels special about this moment, as if it's confirmed what I felt the first time I met Alaric.

"What was that all about?" Astrid asks as she and Cordelia converge on me.

"We were dancing, like we were supposed to." I glance over at Alaric, who has already joined his own friends on the other side of the room. The break won't last long, but we're all making the most of it.

"Mmhmm. It looked more like flirting to me," Cordelia says.

"We're supposed to flirt while dancing," I point out. "It's part of what they're training us to do, remember?"

Astrid laughs. "There's a difference between court flirting and actual flirting."

"Is there? I've never noticed one," I lie.

"I say we don't believe her," Astrid says to Cordelia.

"I'd say so. The way he was looking at her was close to asking her to marry him."

I choke. "Alaric didn't do that," I say quickly.

Astrid raises an eyebrow. "So what did he do?"

I sigh. I suppose they'll learn about what he asked by the end of the day when I don't go with them to dinner. "He asked me to share a meal with him in the village tonight."

"And you said you'd go?" Surprise is evident in Cordelia's voice.

"Yes."

"I can't believe you."

"Why would I lie about that?" I ask, trying not to be too confused.

"That's not what I mean," she says. "You've not said yes to anyone's request for dinner. What's different about him?"

I look in Alaric's direction again. "I don't know," I admit. "You know when you get a feeling about someone and know they're supposed to be in your life for some reason?"

Astrid nods. "It's how I felt the day I met the two of you."

A smile spreads over my face. "Me too. I knew we were going to be best friends for a long time."

"I did as well," Cordelia adds. "I'd just resigned myself to only ever being able to spend time with my sister and never have any other friends, and then the two of you came into my life and changed all that."

"I thought you liked Mati?" I ask. She always talks so highly of her sister.

"I do. But it's not the same as having friends of my own, especially since I left home." Pain flits across her face. I know she doesn't hold it against her sister, but being banished from the sea has taken its toll on poor Cordelia.

I reach out and take her hand in mine, doing the same with Astrid. "I'm so glad I met the two of you."

Before we can continue, the music starts up again and the teacher bangs his cane against the floor. I'm sure he waits for the precise moment that everyone is deep in conversation to do it. Of all the staff in the academy, he's the one who makes me feel as if he's on a power trip when he teaches.

But that means we all have to do precisely what he wants us to.

The three of us get into line along with the rest of the girls in our class. The music starts and we move through the steps. Every time I turn, I try to catch a glimpse of Alaric, but the dance doesn't bring us close together again. It's an unfortunate downside of dance classes that we can't always stick with the same partner, but as this is supposed to prepare us for the formal balls and events in the various kingdoms, the academy likes to mix it up so we practise talking to people we don't know very well.

I guess I'll have to wait for our dinner later to talk to him again. I'm starting to see the appeal of why he wants to go so soon.

I suppose it means we won't drag it out if we're not interested in spending more time together. This time tomorrow, we'll either be moving towards a proper courtship, or we'll have gone our separate ways.

For some reason, I'm not as nervous as I should be.

CHAPTER 2

I flip the page of my book, trying to focus on the words in front of me, but failing miserably. Some of the political subjects they make us learn are particularly boring. Normally when they're about defunct kingdoms that no longer have input into the way the world works.

I suppose the classes may have some relevance for people who are trying to become leaders of their kingdoms.

That's not me. I'm never going to rule my kingdom, and even though I signed up, I have no intention of ruling Bellpoint Castle either.

Though perhaps I should pay more attention so I can help whichever of my two friends wins. I'm sure it's going to be one of them.

"Are you all right?" Astrid asks. "You keep sighing and looking at that book like you want to throw it at the wall."

"I'm just preoccupied."

"The competition?" Cordelia asks.

"Your prophecy?" Astrid almost says over her.

"Neither," I admit.

"You should probably take your prophecy more seriously," Cordelia says. "I've heard of people nearly dying because of them."

I shrug. "I just avoid swans."

"What have they got to do with your prophecy?" Astrid asks.

Uh-oh, now I've gone and done it. Like most of the other students with prophecies, I keep it to myself, even from my friends. We should probably share more, especially as the two of them also have prophecies.

"There's not much to it," I admit, knowing there's no getting around telling them now the conversation is open. "Three cursed swans will appear to me, and after that I have two weeks until I die."

Astrid lets out a squeak. "Die?"

"Mmhmm. See, not much to it."

"You don't know how it's supposed to happen?"

I shake my head.

"But how can you do anything about it if you don't know more?" Cordelia asks.

"There isn't any more. My parents tried to find out more, but everyone they asked told the same story. That's my prophecy. It worried me at first, but then I sort of got over it. I stay away from swans just in case."

My friends stare at me like I've told them something awful, but as far as prophecies go, it's not too bad. Dying is something that happens to all of us. It's not like I'll be cursed to an endless sleep or turned into an animal and enslaved.

I can tell that the two of them don't feel quite the same about it, but I know they'll get there.

"I was actually thinking about dinner with Alaric."

"Did it not go well?" Astrid asks.

"It went great," I counter.

"Then what's the problem?" The confusion is clear on Astrid's face.

"I don't know." I let out a loud sigh. "He was charming and we had a great time..."

"But you don't feel anything for him?" Cordelia finishes.

"Actually, I did. But then at the end of the evening, I thought he was going to kiss me and he didn't."

"Ah, I've had that problem," Astrid says. "It might not be what you think it is."

"You mean he might have had a good time?"

"He might have even wanted to kiss you," Cordelia pipes in. "But he got nervous."

"How do I know if that's the case or if he just isn't that interested?"

"Talk to him," Cordelia says. "You won't get anywhere if you just assume what he's thinking."

Astrid nods along. "Exactly."

I sigh, but before I can ask them more about what they think they'd do in my situation, a servant appears with a letter clutched tightly in her hands.

"I have correspondence for Your Highness," she says, dipping into a curtsy and leaving us no doubt who she's talking to.

"Thank you." I take it from her with a smile to dismiss her. She disappears back to wherever the other servants are waiting to be called by the other students in the room.

"Are you expecting anything?" Astrid asks.

I shake my head. No one ever really sends me letters. If my parents want to tell me something, one of them normally shows up. Our kingdom isn't very far from here and if I'm needed, I just go. It's helpful, but means I don't have much written communication with the outside world.

I tear open the letter, a little excited to finally be getting communicated with.

Elisa,

Meet us in the forest by the lake once night has fallen.

Your brothers.

I frown. It's not the crypticness that confuses me the most, it's the fact that my brothers want to see me at all. They all have their own tasks to attend to and none of them involve checking up on their younger sister.

"What is it?" Cordelia asks.

"My brothers, they want to see me."

"Do you want us to come with you?"

I shake my head. "There's no need. I'm sure it's just a quick visit to let me know something about the kingdom." I'm not completely convinced by my words, but what else is it going to be?

"Why aren't they here anyway?" Astrid asks. "You've never said."

"Oh, Covey and Vireo are too old to attend now anyway. I'm not sure why father never sent Efron here, maybe he hasn't seen the need. He'd be in the year above us."

"And remind me why we haven't met your brothers yet?" Astrid raises an eyebrow. "I've seen your parents, I have no doubt they're handsome and polite. How often do you get that in the same suitor?"

I let out a small snort of amusement despite the seriousness of the letter, and the fact we're talking about my brothers. "I can invite them to the next ball if you'd like." I doubt any of them are looking to court anyone, their schedules are busy enough as they are already. But it doesn't hurt to make an introduction and see if either of my friends has a connection with one of them. I wouldn't mind turning them into my sisters by marriage as well as my sisters through choice.

"You should do that," Astrid says firmly.

Cordelia doesn't look as convinced, but that's unsurprising. She's always been the more reserved of the two of them. Astrid's confidence comes from years of being around her parents' shops, talking to customers and interacting with people on a daily basis. On the flip side, Cordelia grew up underwater away from the practices of our world. I'm sure that if we were amongst other mermaids, she'd have an edge that the two of us don't.

Maybe she'd be good for Efron after all. While Covey and Vireo were born only a year apart, there are three years between Vireo and Efron. He grew up being taught the skills of a prince on his own, unlike my older two brothers. I imagine the two of them may have more in common than either of them first think.

Or maybe not. I can't push them together just because I think they'll be a good match. There's more than goes into two people being a good match.

And what do I know anyway? It's not like I know much more than either of my friends about official courtship. According to my parents, a few people have asked for my hand in marriage, but they turned them down for me when they failed to answer what my favourite colour is. According to my father, he doesn't want me to marry anyone who doesn't take the time to get to know me. Which is all well and good, but no one has *tried* to get to know me.

Until Alaric.

My friends are right, I need to talk to him about what happened between us after our dinner. It should have ended very differently from the way it did, and I'm not happy about it. But that's not just on him, it's on me too.

But before I can do any of that, I need to find out what my brothers need. I close my hand around the letter, scrunching up the paper until it scratches against the soft skin of my palms.

I glance at the clock, disappointed to see that there's still a frustrating amount of time left until I have to meet them.

But that's fine. It can't be super urgent if they're not coming to me now.

I hope.

CHAPTER 3

I pull my cloak tightly around me to stave off the chill which hangs in the air. The wind whistles through the trees, making them sway back and forth in a way that makes it a little too eerie for my liking.

A shiver runs down my spine, but this one has nothing to do with the cold and everything to do with the atmosphere around us.

Why do my brothers want to meet me now?

The more I think about it, the more questions I have. As my family, they're allowed on campus. They could come in the front door and ask for me any time they want. So what's going on that they can't do that?

A branch brushes against my arm, making me jump and let out a small yelp.

The sooner I can get out of the forest again, the better.

Thankfully, the lake appears soon enough and I step into the moonlight. As much as I want it to be better, I'm not sure it is. Splashes from the creatures living in the water break through the night, and the wind is still rattling amongst the trees.

A loud squawk sounds from above.

I jump back, barely holding back the scream which wants to rip from my throat. I'm not doing a good job of being the cool and collected princess I've been trained to be my entire life.

Three huge swans drift down from the sky and land in the lake with a gentle splash as they hit.

Fear runs through me as I realise what this means and the danger it poses to me.

My countdown clock has started.

I want to call out for my brothers, but I know it won't do any good. I can protest, I can run, I can hide, but none of that is going to make a difference to my fate.

The only thing I can possibly do is work out how to stop my prophecy from coming true. I don't know for sure that there's a way to do that, but enough students at Grimm Academy have managed. Hopefully, I can find a way to make sure I'm one of them.

The swans glide over to the edge of the lake and step onto land, each of them shaking the water off their feathers as they make their way towards me.

I'm so in shock that it almost doesn't register when the three birds transform into the people I'm waiting for.

In a cruel twist of fate, my brothers are the swans that foretell my death.

That's got to be a new one.

"Thank you for coming, sister," Covey says, though his normally reassuring tone is lost given the situation.

"What's happening?" My gaze flits between the three of them, waiting to see who will answer. "You haven't always been able to do this, have you?"

"It's a recent development," Vireo mutters under his breath.

A sigh of relief slips from me. I can't imagine my parents would have kept this from me if they'd known. Then again, we chose to keep my prophecy from my brothers so we didn't worry them.

Or so they didn't go around the kingdom killing all the swans in a futile attempt to keep me safe.

"We've been cursed," Covey says.

"To turn into swans?"

"Every day." Vireo's anger is clear on his face. "When the sun sets, we have the option of transforming back into our human forms, but while the sun is up, we're stuck."

My mouth falls open. "What? How? Why?"

"Which do you want us to answer first?" There's wry amusement in Efron's tone despite the situation. I'm not surprised by it, he's always been the one who sees the best in situations, no matter how bad they are. Though I may draw the line at this one.

"Start at the beginning and don't leave anything out," I instruct.

Covey gestures to a cluster of rocks by the side of the lake and the four of us make our way over to them and sit down. I wish I'd known we were going to be sitting, I'd have organised some more seating options.

"We're not sure exactly why this is happening," Covey says once we're all seated. "A witch from a foreign land was visiting and trying to negotiate something with father. We're guessing it went badly, because the next thing we knew, we were cursed to turn into swans every day."

Horror fills me. Is this all because of my prophecy? I know I can't control the actions of others, but it feels like it's my fault. I may not have asked for a prophecy to be placed on me, but without it, perhaps my brothers wouldn't be cursed.

"Is there a way to break the curse?" I ask.

Vireo shrugs. "Not that we've found. But we're limited in where and when we can look."

Ah. That's a good point, and not one I'd considered when I asked the question.

"That's why we came here," Efron says. "We thought you might know the answers."

"We don't study specific curses," I admit, my voice shaking as I realise my brothers are pinning all of their hopes on me.

"But you have access to the academy's library and teachers, right?" Vireo demands.

"Well, yes."

"Then you can find out everything you can." His matter-of-fact tone leaves no room for any arguments.

Not that I want to tell them no. I'll need to research as much as possible so I can work out how I'm going to avoid my prophecy. It doesn't seem outside of the realms of possibility that I'll come across something that will also help my brothers. If I'm lucky, the solution might even be the same.

Perhaps that's a little bit of a stretch, but it's better than believing all four of us are doomed.

What will my parents do then? None of my cousins have been trained in the art of running a country. There's never been much cause to think one of my brothers won't be the next king.

"I can look into it," I promise.

"Thank you," Covey speaks in a gentler tone than my middle brother. Clearly, he's the one who realises how much of my help they actually need.

"I can't promise anything," I remind them. "But I'll do everything I possibly can to make sure I find a way to undo the curse."

Efron smiles weakly at me, not doing a good job at hiding the fear in his eyes. He doesn't have the same confidence my older brothers have, and I'm not sure I blame him. If the situations were reversed I'd be just as scared.

To be fair to myself, I'm scared even with just my part in it. The words are on the tip of my tongue to tell my brothers about my prophecy, but they don't come. The last thing I want to do is worry them any more than they need to be. Especially when they won't be able to do much about it while they're trapped in their swan forms.

Instead, I force a smile onto my face, all while hoping it's reassuring. "We'll fix this," I promise.

"Thank you, Elisa, we knew we could count on you," Covey says.

"That's what family is for. Have you told our parents about this?" I ask.

Their silence tells me everything I need to know. We're keeping them in the dark for now.

It's probably for the best. Mother would spend more time worrying about all of us than actually figuring out the situation, and we'd just distract Father from his job of running the kingdom. Though I suspect having an heir problem would be something worthy of causing a distraction, even if it's bad for us.

"I won't tell them," I promise. "At least not yet. If we haven't been able to find anything out in a month, you'll have to." Especially because there's a good chance I'll be dead if I don't figure this out.

What a cheery thought.

"We will," Efron says. "I know it's best to keep it from them for now, but there's only so long we can keep up the ruse that we've gone on a hunting trip."

I raise an eyebrow. "Is that what you've told them?"

"What else could we do? It's not like we could say we were on some kind of envoy mission and then return with nothing," Covey points out.

A loud sigh escapes me. This is messy to say the least, but I know they're right. Our parents have to stay in the dark and the four of us have to figure this out. It's as simple as that.

We say our goodbyes, though I don't think any of our hearts are really in it. I don't know about them, but I'm already worrying more than I want to about the situation. And not just there's either, I also have my prophecy to worry about.

And the competition to become the heir of Bellpoint Castle. I may not plan on winning, but if I want to help Astrid and Cordelia, then I need to stay in the running for now.

And Alaric.

I need to talk to him about dinner and whether I read the connection between us wrong, but how can I when it involves bringing him into this disaster of a situation?

I push the thought aside. I'll worry about it next time I see him. There's no reason that I can't manage my life, my prophecy, and my brothers' fates.

Probably.

CHAPTER 4

My bedroom door bursts open and my friends bustle in. I groan and pull the covers over my head. There aren't any classes today, and I need to go to the library to see if I can come up with something to help save my brothers.

And me.

"It's time," Astrid announces, dropping herself down onto my bed and pulling away my blanket.

"For what? Breakfast is served for hours yet," I point out.

"It might be, but we don't have time for leisurely food, we need to go to the tent at the front of the academy."

"What? Why? There isn't a special event today?" Have I missed something? I can't recall anything, but maybe it's something that didn't interest me.

"What Astrid is trying to say is that it's the first round of the Bellpoint Castle competition."

I sit up, taking the mug of steamy tea she offers me. "That's today?"

Astrid nods. "There was an announcement after dinner, didn't you see it?"

"No." Probably because I hurried away after eating so I could meet my brothers and avoid talking to Alaric before I dealt with them. Maybe it's not good to run away from all of my problems, but while I didn't know what I was up against, it was the only thing I can do. "You'd think they'd give us a little more warning," I grumble.

"It's their kingdom, they get to do what they want," Astrid points out.

I take a sip of my tea while I think about the best way to answer that. I don't think it's necessarily true. The invitations to sign up are sent to the academies which cater to the nobility and royalty of the various kingdoms. While there are rich merchant children like Astrid who also attend, and at Grimm, there are some scholarship students from poorer families, both groups are in the minority. The people running Bellpoint's competition know who they're dealing with.

Which means that the choice to not give us much notice is purposeful, though I'm not sure why. Maybe they're trying to see who is open-minded enough to turn up.

"How long have we got?" I ask.

"Long enough for you to get dressed and eat the breakfast we grabbed for you on our way down."

"You let me sleep that long?"

My friends exchange a worried glance.

"We knew you were meeting your brothers last night, we figured you needed your sleep. We didn't think you'd oversleep," Cordelia explains.

"Thank you, it was a long night."

"Anything you want to tell us?"

I sigh. "Maybe later, I don't want to distract us all from the competition. That's what we should be focusing on." Especially if we want to make sure one of the two of them wins.

Cordelia looks as if she wants to argue with me, but decides better of it. I'm glad. We can't have too many distractions.

"Do you want us to help you dress?" Astrid asks.

I roll my eyes. "You know I'm perfectly capable."

"It depends what you want to wear. I've seen some of your dresses, and they probably need a whole team to tie you into it," Astrid says. "And before you argue about it, remember my sister is a seamstress."

I let out a small chuckle. "I'm thinking something a bit simpler for today." Especially as I have no idea what's going to happen for the first task. There's no difference between the male and female contestants, but that means I have to be practical.

"We'll wait outside." Cordelia grabs Astrid's hand and pulls her outside. It's probably a good thing, Astrid would stay and probably make some outrageous suggestions of dresses that aren't in the slightest bit suitable for the day ahead.

I get myself ready quickly, and leave my room, heading down to the front lawn with my friends. True to their word, they've brought me a breakfast roll.

Over a dozen students mill around the newly erected tent, most of them not talking to anyone as they nervously wait.

"I'm glad I'm doing this with the two of you," Cordelia says, looping her arms through ours.

"Me too." Though I can't help but think this is a tremendous amount of time I'm not spending in the library looking for answers.

It's hard to choose between my friends and my family.

"Good morning, everyone," a man says from the front of the tent.

Even though there wasn't much noise to begin with, the silence that falls over the assembled students is deafening.

"I'm Master John from Bellpoint Castle and I want to welcome you to the heir competition. As I'm sure you're aware, this competition is being run at academies across the kingdoms. Each task will assess a variety of skills, and they will be used to judge you. The heir will be the person who we deem to be the most suitable. The criteria for that will not be revealed for the purpose of fairness."

I exchange glances with my friends. It's hard to win something if we don't even know how to do it. But I know we'll manage. If they're looking for a leader, then that's what we're going to have to work towards. It should be fairly simple to guess what they want.

"Your first task will be to organise a seating chart for a banquet to honour the coronation of a new monarch. Each of you is going to be given a sheet of parchment including the titles of the people who are being invited, and a map of the banquet hall. You'll have an hour to place everyone in the right seats. Once you've completed the charts, they'll be collected and you can enjoy the rest of your days. We'll contact you all when the next task is imminent," Master John says.

Several servants walk around the room handing out scrolls and a seating chart.

"Thank you," I say as they give one to me.

My friends echo my gratitude.

I glance down at the chart, relieved to see it's the same kind I've been using my entire life. Mother taught me how to set one up when I was ten. I could probably do this with my eyes closed. Though my penmanship would leave a lot to be desired.

"You may begin," Master John announces.

I unroll the scroll and scan the titles on the list. There's a small biography next to each, though no names. Some of them I recognise as real people.

I make sure I know who everyone on the list is first, then work my way through the chart, starting at the head table. I fill in the slots with the various officials, ensuring that there are no clashes between the guests. While some of the information is on the scroll, there are other things to take into account too, like the history between kingdoms and any recent squabbles. It's not the easiest task to achieve without the support of someone whose job it is to keep up to date on these things.

I glance at Astrid only to find her confidently putting people in the right place. Between the information on the scroll, and what her family will have kept up to date on in order to know what to trade with who, she seems to know what she's doing.

Confident that she doesn't need any help, I switch my attention to Cordelia, who seems to be having more trouble with it.

"You can't put these two next to each other," I whisper, pointing at a table on her chart. "Their siblings were married and had a very public divorce. They haven't spoken since."

She nods and leans in to scratch out one of the names. "Thanks. Anything else I should know?"

I scan her chart. "You're doing good so far. But I'll keep checking if you want?"

"I appreciate it. I didn't realise how much I didn't know until now." She bites her bottom lip, something I've seen her do when she's struggling with some kind of problem with our academy work.

"It's all right, we'll get through it together," I promise.

"But only one of us can win."

"I know, but we can increase the chances that it's one of us by working together," I point out.

"Are we even allowed to?"

A frown pulls at my features. "I don't know. They didn't outright say that we can't." But no one else in the tent is talking to one another.

"We'll just make sure that we're not caught," I promise.

Cordelia laughs softly. "That might be easier said than done." She nods towards the front of the room where several of Master John's servants are watching us all with hawk-like gazes.

They've probably already seen the two of us talking.

"If anyone asks, tell them that I was asking you for help and you didn't do anything."

"I'm not going to do that," Cordelia responds. "If they're going to penalise teamwork, then maybe it's not the kind of kingdom I want anything to do with."

A smile spreads over my face at her words. She's not wrong. The kingdom should take pride in someone who knows how to take advice from others.

We work in silence, conscious of the time limit. Every now and again, Cordelia asks me about someone and Astrid does the same, though her chart needs a lot less fixing. By the end, I'm confident that all three of our charts are decent representations of what they should be, and that they're all different.

"That's the end of the task. Please hand your completed seating plans in now," Master John announces.

I sit back and hand over my parchment, mostly confident that we're all going to have passed this round. I'm not sure how it all works, but I imagine they'll let participants know if they won't be progressing to the next round.

They should really have done some kind of orientation. Or maybe they did and I missed it.

"Do you want to head into the village now?" Astrid asks once we've left the tent. "I've heard that the dressmaker has some new fabrics and I want to check them out."

I shake my head. "I need to go to the library. I have an essay I completely forgot about due."

"I'll come with you," Cordelia says. "I want a new dress for the ball next week."

I wave goodbye to my friends and head back up to the academy, determined to find something that can help me and my brothers.

CHAPTER 5

"E lisa!" Alaric calls down the corridor.

I turn to find him rushing towards me.

"Have you been avoiding me?" he asks.

I blink a few times, unsure how to answer. I've not been searching him out, even though I probably should have given the questions I need to ask. But with spending every minute from the past three days I can on trying to find an answer to my brothers' problem, I haven't thought much about what's going on between us.

"I'm sorry, I've been really busy," I say, knowing it's not enough.

"Did I do something wrong? I thought our dinner went well."

I take a shaky breath. "So did I, but then I thought you were going to kiss me and you didn't."

Shock crosses his face. "Oh."

"I'm sorry, I just didn't know what to think, and then something came up with my family, and the Bellpoint competition..."

"I didn't realise you were taking part in that."

"I am, but mostly to help my friends," I admit.

"I wanted to kiss you," he says. "But I didn't want you to think that was all I was interested in when I just want to get to know you."

"I never thought that." I tuck a strand of hair behind my ear.

"Next time, I promise I will. So long as you'll let there be a next time?"

"You haven't asked," I point out.

Alaric chuckles. "You're right, I haven't. That's my mistake. There's a ball coming up next week, would you like to go with me?"

My heart flutters. "I'd love to."

"Great."

Before he can say anything else, the bell that signals the start of the next lesson.

"I need to go." I gesture to the classroom door. "But we can sort the details out later?" I suggest.

"I'll catch up with you later." He leans in and kisses my cheek before hurrying away to a class of his own and leaving me staring after him.

It takes me a moment to remember that I need to go into the classroom in order to attend my lesson. I slip through the door and take my seat while still in a little bit of a daze after my conversation with Alaric. I suppose that's one thing less I have to worry about, but it still leaves a lot behind.

None of the other students pay me much notice, which is fairly normal. I may be a princess, but so are at least five of the other girls in the room,

I don't even want to think about how many there are throughout the kingdoms. Between large families and a lot of kingdoms entered into a peace treaty that allows us all to mix at places like Grimm and the various other academies, there are a lot of royal families and nobility around. I don't mind, it makes me one of many instead of someone to be singled out and treated differently. I much prefer things this way to the alternative. Almost all of our history lessons revolve around the wars and various assassination attempts that went on. Not to mention the marriage pacts that would tear people like me away from their homes and force them into a marriage with someone they never met before.

I much prefer being able to spend my time at Grimm Academy and make my own way in life.

"Good afternoon, class," Miss Friar says.

Silence falls over the room as we turn our attention to her and she starts her lesson. Unlike some of the teachers, she generally manages to make her subject interesting.

"We're going to be talking about fairies today," she announces. "And the etiquette that surrounds dealing with them. Each of the factions is different, so you need to keep that in mind when you're dealing with them."

"Is it possible to tell which faction we're dealing with?" a boy at the front of the class asks.

"Unless they tell you, no," Miss Friar answers, not even skipping a beat. She's never minded questions. She told us in our first class that she thought it helped us learn when we got a chance to interact with the learning material. "And the chances of that are slim at best. If you need the help of the fairies, then you have to be truly desperate."

"What kind of things can they help you with?" a girl at the back says. I think her name is Rebekah, but she has her own group of friends and this is the only class we share, so I don't know for sure.

"Pretty much anything to do with magic," she responds. "But just because you ask them something, it doesn't mean that they'll actually do anything. It's up to the fairies to decide."

"How can you make it more likely that they'll help?" Rebekah asks with a hint of fear in her voice. I don't know whether it's because of the concept of trying to find the fairies, or the consequences of not being able to. I haven't heard any rumours about her having a prophecy, but that's to be expected.

"You can't," our teacher answers. "But your chances are probably better if you take them an offering. Bread and milk is often the preferred tribute, but even that isn't a sure thing. You also have to be as polite as possible."

A soft chatter fills the room as we all absorb the information she's given us.

"Is it true that some of them prefer being around late at night?" someone asks.

"Some do, I believe it's for privacy more than anything else," she says. "But there are plenty of rumours about fairies during the day. The one thing you should always remember when it comes to fairies is that you shouldn't believe everything you hear about them, but you should believe that all of it is possible."

"Is it true that there are fairies in the forest here at Grimm?" the first boy asks.

I perk up, eager to know the answer. If there are, maybe that means I can try and find them. It may not work, but it's worth a try. If I don't find anything, then I'm no worse off than I am now. If I do, then I might be able to end all of this.

Miss Friar chuckles. "I've heard those rumours. But I've never had the pleasure of meeting a fairy, so I can't confirm or deny that. All I can say is that the Grimm forest is full of all kinds of creatures. While safe, there are many mysteries there. If you go looking in the right place, at the right time, you may find fairies. You may also find a lot of other things. It all depends on what wants to find you."

I lean back in my seat and consider everything she's saying. I've seen a map of the forest while in the library before. Maybe if I can locate it again, I can figure out a good place to begin my search for the fairies.

And if they know how to fix my brothers' curse, then I may stand a chance at saving all of our lives.

I glance up in time to see Miss Friar looking at me with a satisfied smile on her face. Maybe I'm imagining it, but it's hard to be sure. The academy isn't allowed to directly interfere with prophecies, but I've heard whispers that they sometimes tailor lesson plans to make sure that students who need certain pieces of information get them.

Maybe the student this lesson has been tailored for is me.

CHAPTER 6

"My lady," Alaric says, holding out his hand so I can place mine on top of it.

A small smile spreads over my face as I go through the necessary motions. Despite everything on my mind, it's nice to have a few hours to myself. If this really is the end of my life, I need to have at least a little enjoyment from it.

We step through the double doors and into the ballroom full of students. One of the announcers calls out our names, but no one pays any attention to them. I'm reasonably sure they do that for the people who would be insulted if they weren't announced properly. But that's not me.

"Would you like to dance?" Alaric asks. "Or we can get some refreshments first if you prefer. Maybe a walk in the gardens." His words almost trip over one another, revealing just how nervous he must be.

I press my spare hand against his arm in what I hope is a reassuring gesture. "I'd love to dance, and then we can do the other things later." Though not *too* much later. I need to sneak out into the forest in a few hours so I can try to find the fairies. A small part of me wants to tell Alaric that, but I can't. The fewer people who are involved in my family's mess, the better.

He draws me onto the dance floor and we fall into position along with all the other couples. I dip into a curtsy while he bows, our gazes locked. I hope the dance they start to play isn't one that will require me to change partners. I want to spend this time with him.

The first chords of the song begin to play, and as one, the assembled students begin the dance. I always wondered why they bothered with dance classes for those of us who have been taking them our entire lives until I attended my first ball at Grimm and realised that the point is trying to make sure all of the students know the same dances for times like this.

Alaric takes my hand in his and spins me under his arm. My skirt flares out, just part of the spectacle for anyone watching. It must really be something to see a ball like this. I've always been more focused on having fun rather than watching to see what it looks like.

"I had a question for you," Alaric says once the dance draws us into a part that allows talking. There are plenty of them, the point of the balls is for us to forge connections and alliances with other students. That's hard if none of us talk to one another.

"Is it whether or not you can kiss me?" I ask.

He chuckles. "No, I was saving that one for later."

"Good to know."

He spins me out, briefly putting a pause in our conversation. He tugs gently on my hand and I turn back, bringing us into a proper hold. Maybe it isn't the proper thing for me to think about, but I love the way his hand feels on my waist. It's reassuring and warm in the best way.

"So, what's your question?" I ask as we fall into a simple box step.

Alaric expertly guides us around the floor, following the couple in front of us.

He clears his throat. "Will you court me formally?"

My eyes widen. Somehow, that's not what I expected.

"I know this isn't the proper way to ask. I should be showering you with gifts..."

"I don't need gifts," I counter.

"Still, it's tradition."

"Then we should make a new one. I don't need gifts to know you're serious when you ask that."

A wide smile makes his whole face light up. "So that's a yes?"

"Yes," I agree. Perhaps I should be saying no given the situation with my brothers and my prophecy, but I can't bring myself to say it, not when he's looking at me the way he is, and making me feel like my whole world feels differently.

"Then there's another question I have to ask you." A serious expression falls over him, like this is the most important thing of all.

"What is it?"

"Would you like to meet my mother? She's visiting the academy next week, and I was thinking that it would be the perfect time to introduce her to the girl I'm courting."

"You want to introduce me to your mother?" I raise an eyebrow.

"Not if you don't want," he says quickly. "I don't want you to be uncomfortable."

I lift my hand from his shoulder, briefly breaking our hold, and place it on the centre of his chest. "I'd love to," I assure him. "I'll just have to make sure I have a suitable gift." I put my hand back on his shoulder so we can continue the dance without causing a surge of gossip.

"You don't have to get her a gift." The echo of my own words isn't lost on me.

"Maybe not, but you're not from my kingdom, I should send for some of the specialities for us." It's a small thing to do, but important if I want to start out this courtship the right way. Making a good impression on his family is important to me.

"You're amazing."

I blush and glance away, not wanting to meet the earnestness in his gaze. Maybe I shouldn't be encouraging whatever this is between us until I have everything sorted with my brothers and my prophecy.

And yet I can't help it. Something about Alaric keeps drawing me to him and making me want to spend more time with him, even if it's the only time I'll ever have.

He guides us too much to the right until we've left the floor.

"What are you doing?" I ask.

Alaric lets go of my waist, but keeps hold of my hand and tugs me into a shaded alcove. We can still see the rest of the students, and if they look in our direction, they'll be able to see us too, but there's still something private and sheltered about the space we've found ourselves in.

"I'm going to revisit the *can I kiss you* question."

Ah.

"Well, we are courting."

"That's not a yes," he points out.

A low laugh escapes me. "I suppose it isn't. But yes is exactly what I mean."

He reaches out and tucks a strand of hair behind my ear. His gaze bores into me, revealing just how much he wants this.

We move closer to one another, both lost in the moment and what it's going to bring for us.

My eyes flutter closed just as his lips brush against mine. I press my hand against his chest as he pulls me closer with a gentle touch on my lower back. I lose myself in the way it feels to be kissed by him, wanting nothing more than this moment to go on forever. More than ever, I'm certain we missed out after our dinner the other night.

But we can make up for lost time now.

We break apart, but don't move from our alcove. I touch my fingers to my lips, still feeling a slight tingle from the pressure.

"I'm sorry that took us so long," Alaric says, his voice hoarse.

"Me too."

"Would you like to dance again?"

I nod. "But only if we can plan for more breaks."

Alaric raises an eyebrow but lets out a small laugh. "I promise we will."

I hold out my hand for him to take so he can lead us back onto the dance floor. There are still a few hours until I need to go and try to find the fairies and I plan to make the most of them, especially if it's going to be bad news when I do. I'm not going to be able to focus on the good things if I get bad news.

Which means I need to take my joy where I can, and right now that means dancing with Alaric and enjoying the rest of the ball before I seal my fate forever.

CHAPTER 7

I hate being in the forest this late at night, but I know there's no choice. While the fairies are always around, they're supposed to be more active at night, and that means this is my chance to talk to them.

I slip my hand into my cloak pocket to check the bread and milk I took from the kitchens as an offering is still there. Despite the fact I'm allowed to ask for things like that, I still feel guilty for having taken it to give to the fairies and not eat myself.

I take a deep breath. It's fine. The academy prides itself in helping students with prophecies. That includes me, even if they don't know that's what's happening.

It's best if I don't think about it too much.

I pull out a copy of the map of the grounds I found in the library while researching. I've never been taught the proper way to draw maps, which means the lines are shaky and the proportions are a little off. But it should be enough to get me to the spot in the forest where the most fairy sightings seem to have taken place.

"Hello?" I call out, hoping to catch the attention of the tiny winged folk. Never having seen one before myself, it's hard to know what I should be looking for. The books have a nasty habit of being wrong about this kind of thing.

I pull my cloak tight against the cool air and try not to worry too much about the possibility of ruining my ball gown. I should be able to get a new one easily enough. New brothers are another matter. They can't be replaced as easily as embroidery and silk.

"My name's Elisa," I call out. "I'm looking for some help and I think you know how to do that. I have an offering." I pull the wrapped bread and the small stoppered bottle of milk out of my pocket and place it by the bottom of the nearest tree.

A small chitter comes from behind me.

I turn, catching my cloak on a branch as I do. I give it a tug, trying not to wince as a rip sounds through the clearing. That's not the most important thing right now.

A small figure floats at eye level in front of me. Her tiny wings are almost invisible in the gloom.

"Good evening, Elisa," she says, her voice louder than I expect it to be given her size. "You've come with an offering, I see."

"I have. I put it by the tree over there, but I can move it if you want me to?" I gesture needlessly.

"That is not necessary. My brothers and sisters will take your offering."

"Does that mean you're going to help me?" Hope wells up inside me.

"No one can help you but yourself," she responds cryptically.

"Oh."

"I know that's not what you want to hear, but the only person able to save you and your brothers is you."

"How do you know what I'm here for?" I ask.

"We know a lot of things," the fairy responds. "We know about your friends and their trials. We know about your family and the problems they are facing, and we know that you would come tonight to ask for our help to rid yourself of your problems."

"But how?"

"Magic, dear Elisa."

"How can I help my brothers? That's what I came here to find the answer to." And if it's the one useful thing the fairy tells me, then it's going to have been worth the trip.

"You're not going to ask about your prophecy first?"

"No. My prophecy coming true is bad news for me, but it doesn't have any real consequences for my kingdom. Leaving my father without an heir is a much bigger potential problem." Even as I say it, I know it's more complicated than that. I don't want to die. "I don't want to lie to you. I'm scared and I don't want to die. But something tells me that my fate is linked to that of my brothers."

"Honesty always goes a long way amongst the fairies," she agrees. "And you are right. If you solve your brothers' curse, then your own prophecy will cease to be a problem for you."

I take a shaky breath. "Thank you." At least that means I can concentrate on fixing this one problem instead of having to figure out how to save my brothers and myself.

"Your brothers' curse is a simple one," the fairy says. You must make them each a shirt made of nettles."

"Nettles?" I echo.

She nods. "Nettles."

"Do they need to be special nettles? Enchanted or picked at a certain time of the month?" I hope the last one isn't going to be the case given that my time is limited."

"No. Just nettles."

"It's really as simple as that? I just have to make them nettle shirts and then get them to wear them?"

"Simple is not the word I would necessarily use," the fairy responds.

Fear flutters through me. What isn't she telling me?

"You must stay silent from the moment you take the nettles we will give you, until your brothers have donned their shirts and broken their curse."

I swallow hard. "What happens if I don't?"

"Your brothers will remain swans, and you will forfeit your life. It is a consequence of the magic you wish to use. You can decide that it does not suit you..."

"No. I'll do it. Is it just verbal silence, or am I also not allowed to write?"

"Verbal silence. Though it goes without saying that you should not tell anyone of the magic you have uncovered."

"I won't," I promise.

"Good. Then you should take the nettles we have provided. Should you need more, the forest will provide them."

"Thank you..." I trail off, realising I didn't ask a simple question that I really should have. "I'm sorry I didn't ask for your name, that was rude of me."

"And I did not supply it," the fairy counters. "And that was by design."

"Oh."

"Fairy folk do not share their names with humans."

"In which case, I'm sorry for asking. If there's anything you require of me in return for your help, please let me know."

The fairy smiled, showing a row of sharp teeth behind her serene features. This is not a creature to be messed with. "Your existing offering is enough," she assures me. "Now take your nettles and leave. Remember you shouldn't speak a word or the enchantment on your brothers' shirts will be broken. We will not cross paths again."

I turn to pick up the basket of nettles she indicates to and turn back to continue the conversation, only to find the fairy has gone. It's probably for the best, I already managed to forget I'm not supposed to say anything. It's going to be difficult to stay silent, even though I know I have to.

I turn to face the tree by which I left the offering, only half surprised to find it gone already. It seems that the fairies move quickly when there's something they want on the line.

Fear thrums within me as I make my way back up the castle with the basket of nettles weighing down on me heavily. One mistake and I'm going to doom us all. My brothers will spend the rest of their lives as swans, and I'll be dead. My parents will lose us all.

Somehow, I need to stop that from happening, even if I'm not sure exactly how. All I know is that I need to get started on the shirts immediately. My time is running out as it is, adding in the fact even one accidental word could end this, and it's cut even shorter.

It turns out that I'm the one responsible for my own prophecy and whether or not it comes true. Hopefully, I have what it takes to not let everyone down.

CHAPTER 8

A slip of paper under my door is the only announcement of the second task for the Bellpoint Castle competition, and the whole thing fills me with dread. Somehow, I need to manage the task without saying a single word.

How am I supposed to help my friends when I can't say anything?

I scrunch my hand into my skirt, wincing as the nettle stings that I've gained from staying up into the early hours of the night stitching and weaving the nettles into shirts for my brothers. I need to be careful no one sees the state of them, or I'm going to end up with questions I can't answer.

I skip breakfast. As much as I don't want to, I have to avoid my friends for as long as possible. They'll know something's wrong, even before they realise I'm not saying anything out loud.

The tent has been put up on the lawn again, and a similar number of students seem to be entering. Either everyone passed the previous round, or they haven't started eliminating people yet.

I hope it's the second one, or I'm not going to stand a chance given my current situation.

I enter and take a seat at one of the small tables and wait for the inevitable arrival of Astrid and Cordelia.

The two of them enter, and stop mid-conversation when they see me already seated. They hurry over and perch themselves on the tables on either side of mine.

"You weren't at breakfast," Cordelia says.

I shake my head and make a gesture to indicate sleep.

"Late night with Alaric?" Astrid raises an eyebrow and smirks.

My eyes widen and I shake my head again.

"Yes, yes, we believe you." She crosses her arms and flashes me an expression that says she doesn't.

I repeat my head shake. This is going to get old very fast. I should have thought about bringing a sheet of paper with me to write on, but given how new the silence is to me, I didn't think about it in time.

Just in case either of them happen to have something in their pockets, I mimic the act of writing with my hands.

Cordelia frowns. "What's wrong with your voice?"

I press my palm to my throat and look as sad as I can, hoping the two of them will just assume I think I'm sick.

"Oh no, maybe you shouldn't be here. We can cover for you?" Cordelia suggests.

"She can't do that," Astrid answers for me. "There's only one chance to compete in this competition. If she doesn't do this task, then she can't move onto the next one and there'll be no way of winning."

"Her health is more important," Cordelia says quietly, making sure to check where the various staff members are so they don't catch on to our conversation. I don't think they'll take very kindly to it.

I reach out and touch my friend's hand gently and nod to try and indicate I'm all right.

"Only if you're sure."

I nod again.

"Fine, but if you end up feeling worse after it, don't come complaining to me," Cordelia says.

I smile reassuringly, resisting the urge to chuckle. I need to be careful not to let myself get too tempted into making any noises. I'm not sure what will count as me speaking, but it's best not to risk it. This isn't some kind of challenge I've set myself, this is a matter of life and death.

"Good morning, all," Master John says, drawing our attention to the front of the tent. "Today's test is simple. You need to prepare appropriate refreshments for a visiting ambassador. You will present them on your tables to be judged. You may begin."

I cover my surprise at the simplicity of the task. And because the customs for this one will vary greatly depending on where each person comes from.

But perhaps that's the point. It isn't just about what we prepare, but how we do it and what spurs us on to make certain decisions.

Around the tent, students get to their feet and make their way over to the various tables, each one laden with the various pots, food, and drinks we'll need.

"Why does this seem too easy?" Astrid mutters.

"I don't think it's supposed to be difficult," Cordelia answers.

I nod along, adding my opinion to hers without saying a word.

"It's supposed to help them judge the best candidate for the heir of Bellpoint Castle, not be unbeatable."

"I suppose that makes sense," Astrid agrees. "But how do we make sure to impress?"

Cordelia shrugs. "I'm going to make up a welcoming tea like I would at home, but adapt it with what I've learned since coming onto land. I remember how the two of you reacted to seaweed tea, I'm not going to make that mistake again."

Amusement dances through me at the memory. It had tasted awful, but Cordelia had been in her element.

Astrid sighs. "That's what I was afraid of. I don't think my go-to tea plans will be right for the situation."

I reach out and place a reassuring hand on her arm.

"Thanks," she says, seeming to understand what I'm trying to say.

Once a little more space has been cleared by the tables, the three of us make our way over and start taking stock of what's there. I don't want to start grabbing things without getting a proper sense of what's on offer, especially when there's so much at stake here. Not just for me, but also for my friends.

Astrid reaches out for an ornate teapot, but I reach out and grab her wrist, shaking my head vigorously. It's a bad choice. Something like that is only ever meant to be used in a decorative capacity.

"What about this one?" She sets her hand on one of the other teapots. It's less ornate, but that makes it a better choice.

The one next to it is even more perfect though. I glance around and make sure none of Master

John's servants are watching me before I pick it up and press it into her hands with a nod.

She looks relieved and hurries it back to her table, setting it down before returning to find the other pieces she needs.

Satisfied that she's off to a good start, I turn my attention to Cordelia. Even from here, it's easy to see she's more at home with the equipment needed to put on a formal tea. She's picking up cups and turning them over in her hands, checking the weight and feel of them all.

She'll be just fine, especially because she'll be combining her traditions with those that have been taught to her at Grimm. I've been around long enough to know that's the kind of thing people love. The mix of old traditions and new will charm most ambassadors, especially when it comes to someone as charismatic as Cordelia. I've seen her charm rooms full of people, even those who are unsure of her heritage as a mermaid. I still don't fully understand why some people have a problem with that. It's not like she chose it.

I pull myself out of my thoughts and start selecting the tea settings I want. I need to do enough to try and pass this round, but I don't want to outshine either of my friends. They don't just need this more than me, but they deserve it too.

I've never been more certain of anything.

CHAPTER 9

I push the needle through the woven nettles, wincing as they sting my fingers, a constant reminder of the weight of what I'm doing and how important it is to get it right. I'm not sure how precisely I need to make the shirts, but it seems like it's better to err on the side of caution and make them as accurately as possible.

The fire crackles in the grate, the warmth from the flames spreading through me and offering at least a little bit of comfort despite the seriousness of my current predicament.

I lose myself in the rhythm of what I'm doing, managing to attach a full sleeve to the first shirt. There's a lot more to do, but I can already feel my confidence growing and the amount of time it's taking me to achieve each part of the process.

A knock breaks through the silence of the room, making me jump and prick my finger with the needle. It barely registers as an annoyance given the stinging I'm used to.

I open my mouth to call out for the visitor to come in, but snap it shut as I realise I can't say anything.

I stick my needle in a pincushion and cover my basket of nettles with a blanket. I have no idea who is on the other side of the door, so it's best that I keep everything as hidden as possible. I make my way over to the door, my whole body thrumming with nerves who may be open on the other side. As far as I know, Cordelia is spending the evening with her sister, while Astrid said she was busy, but not what with. I trust she'll tell us in due course. They also believe I'm sick and resting.

My palm smarts as I wrap my hand around the door handle and pull it open. My eyebrows shoot up at the handsome face staring back at me. I've not been avoiding Alaric, but I also haven't told him any of what's going on.

"I didn't see you at dinner," he says. "I thought I'd bring you some food and see if you wanted any company. Don't worry if you don't, I can go..."

I cut him off with a shake of my head and step back. It's probably foolish to let him in when I can't speak. I'm tempting fate by spending time with him, but my hands need a rest and I do want to see him.

He makes his way over to the desk and lays out the contents of his basket. The delicious smell of fresh-baked bread fills the air, and I'm glad to see he's also brought some of the kitchen's ham and creamy goat's cheese. My stomach rumbles, reminding me that I shouldn't be skipping meals, even if it means I can spend more time working on the shirts for my brothers.

"I didn't know what you'd want, so I brought a little of everything," he says, pulling out a bottle of ginger ale and pouring two glasses.

I flash him a grateful smile, wishing I could thank him with words. It goes against all the training my parents ever gave me not to say anything about such a thoughtful display.

"Is there a reason you're not talking to me?" he asks.

I start to lift my hand to my throat to make the same gesture laden explanation I gave to my friends, but something stops me. I don't want to lie to him. I'm uncomfortable enough having done it to Astrid and Cordelia. I'll explain it all to them when I'm able to speak again.

Instead, I hold up a finger to ask him to wait for a moment and set down the goblet he just gave me so I can open my desk drawer and take out the things to write with. I scrawl the word *prophecy* across it. I hold it up for him to read.

"Oh. I didn't realise you had one," Alaric says.

I grimace and nod at the same time.

"I'm sorry."

I set my paper down and shrug.

He sucks in a sharp breath. "What's happened to your hands?"

I glance down at them, unsurprised to find them splotchy and red from the nettle stings. I resist the urge to hide them behind my back. He's seen them now, the damage is done. Instead, I gesture to the piece of paper again.

"Ah, I see. The gardener at home used to make a salve for her hands, I can write to her and see if she'll send me the recipe? I'm not sure if it'll help if it's a magical issue, but it might be worth a try," he suggests.

I nod eagerly.

"I'll do that. Do you want me to go?"

I shake my head and gesture to the chairs by my fire. I'm lucky to have a room big enough for them, not everyone does.

Alaric smiles and makes his way over along with a plate of food.

I grab my own, and head over to join him. The blanket covered basket of nettles taunts me from beside my chair, urging me to do more work on them. But I'm not sure whether working on the shirts in front of Alaric will break the enchantment, and I can't take the risk. Not when something so important is on the line.

But it's fine. I'll enjoy some time with him and once he's left, I'll start work again.

"Is there anything I can do to help with your prophecy?" he asks.

I shake my head. I wish it wasn't the case but I think I have to go through this on my own.

To my surprise, Alaric reaches over and takes my hand in his, giving it a brief squeeze. "If you change your mind, all you have to do is say the word and I'll be there to do whatever it is you need me to. I don't imagine it's fun to go through this alone."

A wave of affection surges through me at his words.

The two of us lapse into companionable silence. Without me being able to verbally add to the conversation, we're limited in what we can talk about, but for some reason that doesn't make the situation feel weird. Quite the opposite. There's an easiness between us that I've only ever experienced with Astrid and Cordelia before. Like them, it seems that Alaric is supposed to be in my life.

I have no idea how long the two of us spend sitting by my fire. My only focus is on the new sense of peace settling within me. The basket is a constant reminder of what I need to do, but for the first time today, I feel as if it isn't something immediate.

It's only once Alaric kisses me goodbye that I re-take my seat and focus everything on the one task, but this time, I'm refreshed and more determined than ever.

I have too much to live for to let this chance slip through my fingers. I'm going to save me and my family. There's no room for failure.

CHAPTER 10

I scrunch my hands up in the skirts of my dress, glad the salve Alaric sent for works, but instead, I'm worrying about the fact I'm an arm short of finishing my brothers' shirts, which means I have to meet Alaric's mother without actually being able to talk. It feels like a disaster waiting to happen.

But I promised him I would meet her, and so I shall.

I reach out and tug on his sleeve until he looks at me and registers the questioning expression on my face.

"I told her that you've had to take a vow of silence. I know it's not good to lie, but I didn't know what else to say. I didn't think you'd want to tell anyone about your prophecy."

I nod my agreement. It's not the best impression to make on his mother, but I don't have any other choice. Even telling Alaric about my prophecy is a step further than a lot of people would ever go.

But I trust him, and I know he isn't going to use the information against me.

He slips a hand into mine and gives it a squeeze. "We'll be all right," he promises. "She's going to understand. I'll tell her you'll be able to speak if she visits in another month. Do you think that'll be enough time?"

I nod again. If I haven't managed to finish the shirts by then, I'll be dead and it'll be a moot point.

A shiver runs down my spine at the thought. I don't want that to happen, not when I have so much I still want to do and see. I want to be there to see my brothers become the men they're meant to be, to see one of my friends crowned as the heir of Bellpoint Castle, and I want to spend more time with Alaric. But more importantly, I want to discover what I can do with my life once I'm free of the prophecy which shackles me.

A large black carriage travels down the main drive towards the academy, pulled by a team of majestic horses. Alaric stiffens beside me, though I'm not sure he's aware of it. I've not had much of a chance to ask him about his relationship with his family. It isn't information he's volunteered, and while I can't speak to ask questions about it, I haven't been able to start a conversation about them.

The only thing I know is that he wants me to meet his mother. Though maybe that's because he wants the support of having someone with him.

I bite my bottom lip, trying to resist the urge of cursing the fairies. I know they've only passed on the knowledge about the way to break my brothers' curse, and aren't the ones who made the criteria, but it's still so trapping to not be able to speak any of the thoughts in my head out loud.

Which is probably the whole point of the enchantment. The shirts could be made of anything, it's my willpower that's being tested.

"Ready?" Alaric asks.

I flash him a weak smile, bereft of any other response. I don't think I'd be ready if I could talk either.

The carriage comes to a stop and the driver jumps down from his seat to make his way to the door. I can feel my frustration at the situation growing even more. I know from experience what kind of people don't open their own doors. Even my parents do it themselves, and they're reigning monarchs rather than a medium-sized noblewoman like Alaric's mother is.

Frills of excess lace proceed the woman in question. It only gets worse once she's more in view. Jewels glitter from within every fold of cloth, but even from this distance, I can tell most of them are fake imitations of the real thing. I hope she isn't wearing them for my benefit.

"Mother," Alaric greets, bowing immediately.

I raise an eyebrow. That's an odd thing for him to do when this isn't a formal event.

"Son," she responds stiffly, not even dipping her head.

I use all of my training to ensure I have a serene smile on my face rather than the scowl I want to let show.

"This is Princess Elisa," Alaric introduces as he lifts the hand holding mine. "We're currently courting."

I smile as warmly as possible and dip into a deep curtsy. Technically, I don't have to do this. Even if I'm not the princess of Alaric's family's kingdom, I still technically outrank both of the other people present. While Alaric can be exempt from a formal greeting in situations like this because of our courtship, his mother isn't.

Not that I expect her to curtsy to me. It's clear she has absolutely no intention of doing any such thing.

"My son tells me you can't speak," she says stiffly.

I nod.

"I suspect that's a blessing for us both," she mutters.

"Mother," Alaric warns.

The woman turns to him, rising to her full height with a look of extreme displeasure on her face. "I've done what I promised and met her, now you can send her away so we can deal with the business we need to."

"I thought you could get to know one another." His hand squeezes mine a little too hard.

I stroke my thumb over his, hoping it helps reassure him that whatever he's finding difficult, I'm around to support him for. It seems like he needs me.

"That's going to be difficult when she can't talk," the woman responds. "So send her away."

Alaric opens his mouth, but I step forward and place a gentle hand on his arm. He turns to face me, a pained expression on his face.

Our gazes lock and I hope he reads my acceptance of the situation in my eyes. I lean in and kiss his cheek before turning away so I can curtsy to his mother again and head back into the academy. I know when I'm not wanted, and that's fine. I can spend the spare time on the shirts.

"I don't like her," Alaric's mother snips once she thinks I'm out of earshot.

I let her comments slide off me.

The feeling is completely mutual.

CHAPTER 11

I hold up the third shirt and study my handi-work. All I need now is to finish the collar and then I'll be done. The only thing left will be to wait for my brothers, but I've already sent them a message that they should come by each night just in case I'm finished. I don't want to take any chances with breaking the enchantment after the shirts are finished.

I set the shirt down and reach for the basket of nettles, only for my hands to come up empty.

I curse silently, much more at ease with being able to stay silent than I was a week ago. My friends have grown used to it too, though I think it's been helping that both of them have been busy. Once my prophecy is over, the three of us are going to have to sit down and have a nice chat over some tea and cakes. I miss being able to talk to them.

At least they know this is about my prophecy now. I didn't want to admit it at first, but when I realised how long it was going to take me to finish the shirts, I knew I had no choice. The longer the situation continued, the more likely they were to think they'd done something wrong, when it has nothing to do with them.

I push those thoughts from my mind. The sun is still shining, which gives me the perfect chance to go collect some nettles and finish the collar of the shirt before nightfall. It'll be good to have this over and done with.

I tidy away everything, making sure the blanket is over them so the maids and anyone else who may feel the need to enter my room doesn't notice them and do something to them. If I could get away with it, I'd consider carrying the shirts with me everywhere I go in order to stop anything from happening to them.

I swing my cloak over my shoulders and fasten it tightly, making sure to pull the hood up so it takes anyone watching a moment to realise it's me. I hate the idea that I have to hide who I am from someone at the academy, but I've heard enough rumours about members of the student body being responsible for another student's prophecy. Even worse are the whispers that some of the staff have also hastened them along.

Tempting fate isn't in my best interest.

I slip the basket over my arm and hurry out of my room, locking it as I leave. No one pays me any attention as I leave the castle, which doesn't surprise me. Everyone is far too busy paying attention to their own problems to think twice about me hurrying towards the edge of the forest.

It only takes me a few minutes to locate a patch of nettles. Did the fairies help make it grow in an obvious place for me? Once I'm finished with the shirts, I plan on taking another offering to them to say thank you, but I doubt I'm ever going to see a fairy ever again. What Miss Friar told us about them implies that they'll only show up for people when they're needed.

I'm sure they'll appreciate some milk and bread regardless.

The hairs on the back of my neck prickle as if I'm being watched. I turn around, scanning the surrounding trees for any sign that someone is there. Nothing attracts my attention, but the feeling doesn't go away.

Maybe it's the fairies after all.

I check again, just to make sure I'm not missing anything obvious. No doubt I'm just spooked because I'm so close to ending all of this. I shake my head to rid myself of any lingering sense of unease and focus my attention on gathering nettles.

That's what I'm here to do, the sooner I complete my task, the sooner I can put the finishing touches to the last shirt.

I glance up at the sky, surprised to find it has darkened since I left my room. It must be later than I thought. Which means I need to get a move on if I want to finish the shirt before my brothers arrive.

The soft ground gives easily beneath my knees, and I dread to think about the mud stains which will be seeping into my gown. I should have thought about this before I came out to collect nettles, but it's too late for that now.

I should have brought gloves too.

Another thing it's too late for.

I suppose I could go back to my room for them, but I'm here now, and it's not like my hands are in great shape anyway. The nettles have taken their toll on them.

I collect enough nettles for the collar but end up hesitating for a moment. I'm reasonably confident that I'll be able to make it with what I've gathered, but what if something goes wrong?

Not wanting to take the risk, I collect a few more of the nettles and settle them in my basket, confident that I'll be able to deal with anything that comes my way.

I get to my feet and turn away from the forest in time to catch the blur of someone moving a few feet away from me.

A chill runs through me as I resist the urge to call out. It's probably nothing to worry about. The Huntsmen run drills daily in the forest on the academy grounds, no doubt it's one of them making their way through a training exercise.

Even thinking up a reasonable explanation does nothing to convince me that there's nothing to worry about, but the only way I'm going to be able to put my mind at ease is if I hurry back to my room and lock myself in.

I glance over my shoulder, half expecting to find someone waiting behind me.

Unsurprisingly, I don't.

I take a deep breath in an attempt to steady my nerves. It's nothing. I'm just on edge because I'm so close to finding out whether my hard work is going to pay off.

Everything will be better once I give the shirts to my brothers, I'm sure of it.

CHAPTER 12

I turn the corner to the corridor where my room is and stop cold in my tracks. My door is wide open, swinging in the light breeze coming from the window.

I slip my hand into my pocket to check my key is there, only to be greeted by the familiar cool metal.

But if I definitely locked my room when I left, who is in there now?

The urge to call out is strong, but I suppress it, knowing I can't let everything end just because I'm a little bit scared.

I take a deep breath, reassured that my brothers will arrive soon, and with darkness falling, they'll be able to change back into their human selves and protect me from any attacker.

The thought manages to still some of the nerves fluttering in my chest.

I approach with caution, only stepping into my room when it appears there's no one in there. A quick glance towards my chair reveals that the blanket covering the nettle shirts is untouched.

Satisfied that it's all part of my imagination, I turn to close the door, only to freeze in my tracks by the satisfied face of a woman I wish I didn't recognise.

"Hello, Elisa," Alaric's mother sneers.

I glance at the door, as if hoping he's about to walk in and diffuse the situation.

"I hope you're not relying on my son to come and help you. He has no idea I'm here."

Then why *is* she here? She doesn't seem to be particularly interested in getting to know me. She wasn't even lying earlier when she said that it wasn't going to be possible to while I can't talk.

I step back, heading towards the window, though I don't know why. We're too high up the building for it to be an actual escape route.

"So, I take it the reason you're not talking is nothing to do with any vow?" she asks.

Technically, I think I could call it a vow, but I know that's not what she means.

"I know all about Grimm Academy and their promise of helping students avoid their prophecies. If I was going to make a wager, I'd say you were one of those students, is that right?"

I gulp, but nod anyway. There's no point lying to her when she's already figured it out, and maybe she'll stop if I admit it.

Somehow, I don't believe that's true.

"And you've dragged my son into it. Did you really think I was going to be able to let that go?"

My eyes widen and I shake my head, wanting her to know that I haven't done anything to endanger Alaric. I never would.

A loud honk sounds from outside my window, making both of us jump.

I half turn to find three swans darting towards me.

A quick glance over at Alaric's mother confirms she's been just as distracted.

Seizing my chance, I throw open the window and dive towards the blanket, pulling it off the shirts. One of them is still missing the collar, but I'm going to have to hope that it's enough.

Before I can pick up the first shirt, Alaric's mother grabs hold of me and pins me to the floor, her hand around my neck.

I claw at her skin, trying to get her to let go.

"Beg and I'll let you live," she sneers. The glint in her eyes says something different. It's as if she knows that getting me to speak is going to make the difference between life and death.

I struggle against her, refusing to say a word.

"Elisa? Are you all right?" Alaric's voice calls from outside the room.

Relief rushes through me, swiftly followed by horror. I don't want him to see his mother like this. I try to push her off, but she doesn't seem particularly bothered by my attempts.

The flap of a white feather by my head announces the arrival of my brothers in the room.

My normally large feeling room suddenly feels small between the three swans and the two of us, soon to have Alaric in the mix too.

"Mother? What are you doing? Get off her!" Alaric shouts.

"She is *going* to speak for you."

"That's not the way to manage it," he counters, trying to pull her away. The swans join him in trying to get her away from me.

Our eyes meet over her shoulder. I do my best to shake my head and look over at where the shirts are lying on the floor.

For a heart-stopping moment, I don't think he's understood, but then he heads over to them and picks one up.

The hand leaves my throat, leaving me gasping for air. I want to cry out and tell Alaric what to do with the shirts, but I know I can't say anything until my brothers are all wearing them.

One of the swans manages to put himself between me and Alaric's mother, spreading his wings so that there's more of a barrier.

"Three swans?" Alaric mutters. "And three shirts?" The moment it clicks is clear on his face.

The swan closest to him holds out his neck and Alaric slips it over.

"What are you doing? Stop that," his mother demands.

"No." He holds his head up high even as the swan's second wing goes through the arm.

Magic swirls around the majestic bird, transforming him back into the human form of my eldest brother.

Tears spring to my eyes. We may just be able to do this. All we have to do is get the other two shirts on my other brothers before I say anything and then we'll all be free.

Alaric's mother has other ideas and leaps forward, only to be stopped in her tracks by Covey.

Alaric throws one of the shirts to me so I can put it on the swan in front of me while he helps the third and Covey keeps a watch on the older woman, who doesn't seem to know what to do now there are so many people around to witness what's going on.

Hastily, I slip the shirt over the swan's neck and ease his wings through the arms, only noticing when the shirt is on that it's the one without a collar.

I cross my fingers and hope with everything I have that it's going to be enough.

The same magic that surrounded Covey surrounds the swan, which helps my nerves a little. I shuffle back to give my brother more room to work.

"No!" Alaric's mother shouts. "You don't know what you've done."

To my surprise, her frustration seems to be aimed at Alaric and not me.

I carefully get to my feet and scan the room, realising that all three of my brothers are standing in their human form, no worse for the lack of collar on the third shirt.

"I did it," I whisper, then wait for a moment to be sure nothing bad is going to happen. When nothing does, I let out a shocked laugh. "I did it," I repeat.

"You can talk again?" Alaric asks, relief written all over his face.

"Of course she can talk again, she reversed the curse on her brothers," his mother spits.

"How do you know about the curse?" Anger flits across his face as he searches his mother's face for the answer.

She laughs loudly, sending a shockwave of discomfort through me. She doesn't seem like the kind of woman to mess with.

"She's the one who cursed us," Covey says.

The horror on Alaric's face says it all.

I hurry over to him and take his hand in mine. "It's not your fault," I whisper.

"I had no idea."

"I know," I assure him.

"I'm going to get the guards," Vireo says gruffly. "Make sure she doesn't leave," he instructs my other brothers.

Covey steps in front of the door, while Efron watches the woman warily.

"These are my brothers," I say, realising the tension in the air needs breaking somehow.

"I guessed," Alaric admits, his voice a little shaky.

It doesn't take long for Vireo to return with some of the academy guards, who quickly take Alaric's mother between them.

"The headmistress would like to see you, Princess Elisa, Lord Alaric," one of them says before they exit the room.

My eyes widen. "How does she know?"

He shrugs. "She told us to be ready nearby tonight. She knows a lot of things. I wouldn't keep her waiting if I were you."

I nod, unsure what else I can do. "We should go," I say to Alaric. The sooner this part is over, the better.

"Thanks for saving us," Efron says, pulling me into a tight hug. "We owe you."

"You're my brothers. You don't owe me anything," I point out. "Though I do have a friend who wouldn't mind a dance at the next ball," I add, thinking back to how well suited I think Efron and Cordelia would be.

"Anything for you, sister," he responds.

Covey and Vireo each pull me into a hug of their own, the relief of this being over rolling off all four of us.

"We can't tell our parents," Covey says.

"We have to. They know about my prophecy."

All three of them stop in their tracks and stare at me.

Oops.

They still have no idea about that.

"I have a prophecy about me. No, had. I think it's over now. I'll tell you more about it later. But we have to tell Mother and Father so they stop worrying about us all. But we can do it together," I assure them.

For a moment, it seems as if Covey is going to argue, but he ends up just nodding. "Fine. We'll tell them over family dinner. Maybe you can introduce Alaric to them at the same time to take some of the attention away."

I let out a small chuckle. "I'm sure that can be arranged. But we really should go see the headmistress. If she's already waiting for us, then we don't want to waste too much time."

He nods. "We'll head home. Thank you, Elisa."

I watch them go, unable to control the relief flooding through me.

"We should get this over with," Alaric says.

I slide my hand into his. "Yes, let's."

This time, I double and triple check I lock my bedroom door again, though it's not as important as it was before, I don't want to make the same mistake twice.

CHAPTER 13

The headmistress looks surprisingly serene given the situation, almost as if she expected to be called to the office by my prophecy.

I glance at the door, wishing Alaric was on this side of it with me. I could do with the support of someone who cares about me right now.

"I'm sure you have a lot of questions," the headmistress says.

"I didn't want to cause any problems for anyone," I say hurriedly.

She smiles reassuringly. "I know. None of the prophecy students do. I think most of you would rather your lives never became entwined with the magic of the prophecies."

"Then why do they choose us?"

"I wish I had the answer for you," the headmistress says. "But some things remain a mystery no matter what we do."

"Then how do we know that my prophecy really is over?" I ask.

"Does it *feel* like it is?" she asks.

I nod. "But I can't explain why."

"Neither can I. But the book of prophecy says your prophecy has been diverted too." She turns a large open book towards me.

A page with my name at the top of it greets me. I scan the details, surprised to learn it has all the information I've ever been given about my prophecy, along with a note that it's been diverted.

"How is this..."

"I don't have an answer for that either," the headmistress says, cutting me off. "When a student with a prophecy enters Grimm Academy, a page appears for them. We're not allowed to share the information with students until after the prophecy has been stopped, or there could be grave consequences. But I can confirm that so far, everything I've read from the book has turned out to be true."

"Oh." I sit back in my seat and touch my hand to my throat. It's odd to be speaking out loud after a week or so of silence and I can already tell I'm starting to lose my voice for real. "What happens now?" I ask.

"Nothing. You can continue your education here, or you can ask your parents to recall you from Grimm Academy. The choice is yours."

"I don't want to leave," I admit, thinking of my friends and of Alaric.

"Then you don't have to. We'd be glad to have you remain with us as a student."

I breathe a sigh of relief. While I haven't admitted it to anyone, I've always worried about having to leave once my prophecy was over.

"I do have one question," I venture hesitantly.

"Hmm?"

"Why did Alaric's mother curse my brothers in the first place?" I'm not sure what answer I'm expecting. Perhaps my brothers did something that meant they deserved to get cursed, but I doubt it. Is the idea of Alaric's mother purposefully trying to hurt me any better, though?

The headmistress sighs sadly. "You're not the first person she's done this to. We've already received word of half a dozen similar cases over the past century."

My eyes widen. "I'm missing something."

"She's a sorceress. A powerful one at that, and she's been cursing siblings to trap the youngest into a spell that would sap them of their youth and beauty to feed her own."

"That's awful," I whisper.

"It is." Something in her tone suggests this isn't the first time something like this has happened at Grimm Academy. "And before you worry about it, I very much doubt Alaric knew anything about it."

"I never thought he did." I saw his face when he realised his mother was behind everything. Unless he is the best actor in all the kingdoms, he had no idea.

"Good. Is there anything else I can help you with?" she asks.

I shake my head.

"Then you can go. If you think of anything else, my door is always open." The smile on her face suggests that's true. "If you could send Alaric in once you leave, it would be appreciated."

"Thank you, I'll send him in." I rise to my feet and dip into a small curtsy. I don't think I need to, but it's nice to be able to show respect to people who deserve it. I turn towards the door, preparing to leave when I think of something else. "What will happen to Alaric's mother?" I ask.

"She'll be dealt with in the proper manner," she responds. "And won't be able to bother anyone again."

That sounds ominous, but I don't want to pry any further and slip through the door.

Alaric jumps to his feet the moment he sees me and rushes over. "Did everything go all right?" he asks.

I nod. "She just took me through what it all means and what happens now."

"And? Do you get to stay at Grimm?"

"Yes."

Relief rushes over his face. "I was really worried they'd make you leave."

I reach up and touch his face lightly. "Even if they did, do you really think that would be the end of us?"

"My mother did just try to kill you."

"And get my brothers stuck as swans," I add. "It wouldn't have been a great day for my parents if you hadn't shown up when you did."

"I'm to blame for bringing her into your life."

I shake my head. "No, you're not. She cursed my brothers before we went on our first dinner. This has nothing to do with you." Though even as I say it, I realise that might not be true. We had already met by that point.

But it's probably something we won't ever get the answer to.

"The most important thing is that I don't blame you," I whisper. "And you shouldn't either."

He nods. "I'll work on it."

"I'll help," I promise. "The headmistress wants to talk to you now too."

"Probably about the awful things my mother did," he mutters.

"Or maybe she just wants to check that you're all right too. That wasn't easy for you either," I point out.

"Hmm."

I go up on my tiptoes and press a kiss on his cheek. "Go on. I'll be waiting here for when you're done," I promise.

He offers me a weak smile as he slips into the office. Despite Alaric's loss of faith, I can tell deep within that it's all going to turn out well in the end. We just have to keep moving forward and not dwell on the past.

It'll take time, but it will be worth it.

CHAPTER 14

The sound of a piece of paper slipping under my door elicits a groan of frustration from me. Can't I even get one day's peace after nearly losing my life?

I get up from my seat and scoop the paper off the floor, flipping it over.

Ah. It turns out it isn't a summons to the next round of the competition. More like the opposite. I've been disqualified. It's not that much of a surprise given how distracted I've been dealing with my prophecy.

I sigh and drop the letter onto the desk. I'll deal with it properly later if I need to.

The door bursts open a moment later, revealing Astrid and Cordelia on the other side, both looking a little out of breath.

"You can talk again?" Astrid blurts, directing a maid to set down a tray of tea.

I chuckle. "I can, yes."

"Then you need to tell us absolutely everything," she instructs. "Start at the beginning and don't leave anything out."

Cordelia hands me a teacup and points to the empty chair.

I take a seat and launch into everything that's happened, making sure I cover everything I can.

"I'm sorry that I didn't tell you straight away," I say once I'm done. "I wanted to, but I didn't want to put either of you in danger. And I didn't know *how* to say it. I know we haven't really talked about our prophecies much."

"We should change that," Astrid says quietly. "Because I also have something to admit about prophecies."

"Oh?" I try to keep the surprise out of my voice.

"I, erm, managed to stop mine last week."

I glance at Cordelia, who seems equally surprised. "You stopped your prophecy?"

She nods. "It's why I ended up kicked out of the Bellpoint Castle competition. I wasn't paying enough attention, even after you helped me with the tea set up."

"Wait, you're out of the competition?" I can't believe how much I've missed by being locked up in my room making nettle shirts.

Astrid frowns. "Yes, earlier this week."

"I'm sorry."

She shrugs. "Don't be. Conan finally asked me if I'd officially court him, so it was worth it."

"The same Conan you keep dancing around because you're worried your parents will expect you to come home engaged to a noble?" I ask.

Astrid sighs. "Yes, but I've decided that I don't care. And if they do, then I'll just convince one of you to give me a title once you're the heir to Bellpoint Castle," she announces.

"That will be up to Cordelia."

"You have as much of a chance of winning as I do," the mermaid counters.

"I really don't. I got my rejection letter just now." I nod to where it's sitting on my desk. "I imagine they weren't too impressed by me worrying about my prophecy either."

"This doesn't bode well for me," Cordelia mutters.

"Which is why we're going to change how we've been doing things," I say. "We're going to make sure you win."

"And that you don't fall afoul of your prophecy either," Astrid adds.

"Exactly. And now the two of us aren't going to be taking attention away from you while you're completing the tasks, it's going to be even better. You'll shine so brightly, no one will ever be able to look past you."

Cordelia laughs nervously. "You don't know that. I have all the other contestants at the other academies to beat too."

"But none of them have your secret weapon," Astrid points out. "Us."

To my surprise, Astrid's reassurances seem to have worked, as Cordelia starts to relax. "You really think I stand a chance of winning this?"

"I've thought as much from the beginning," I admit.

"Me too. And it'll be good for you and Matilda if you win too," Astrid adds.

Cordelia sighs. "I know. Mati's been amazing, and Lewis has been trying his best to accommodate both of us, but I don't think he meant to gain a little sister when he proposed to Mati. It would be good to be the one providing for myself."

"Even more reason for us to make sure it happens," I say.

Astrid raises her teacup. "To Cordelia, the future Queen of Bellpoint Castle."

"To Queen Cordelia," I say, raising my own.

The three of us chink our teacups together sealing what I know is going to be a great alliance on top of an amazing friendship.

A small smile spreads across my face as I consider the two young women in the room with me. Each of us has our strengths and our weaknesses, but together, we're learning to overcome them.

I should have trusted in that when it first became clear that my prophecy was coming to pass, and I regret not turning to the two of them for help in the first place. But I've already learned from that.

I can trust my friends with my life. And I hope I can prove to them that the same is true. Especially as we do everything in our power to make sure Cordelia becomes the heir of Bellpoint Castle.

And now neither Astrid or I have our own prophecies to worry about, we'll have even more time to be able to put towards making it happen.

"Oh, there was one thing I forgot to mention," I say, pulling my friends' attention to me. "I got Efron to agree to come to the next ball. Call it payment for making sure he didn't spend the rest of his life as a swan."

Astrid snorts. "I think he owes you more than one ball."

I shake my head in bemusement. "Maybe, but I'm not about to hold this over my brothers. I didn't ruin my hands so I could hold it over them. But I do think we might be able to convince Efron to study here for a bit." After the stress of the curse, it'll probably be good for him to spend some time around people his own age.

"I guess we need to make sure Cordelia is looking radiant in her ballgown then," Astrid says.

Cordelia doesn't look completely opposed to the idea.

The three of us lapse into easy conversation about the best fabrics and colours to suit Cordelia's complexion, recovering our familiar ease from before my prophecy took over my life.

Considering my family is safe, I'm courting someone wonderful, and my friendships have survived, I'd say the prophecy failed on every level.

Now I get to enjoy the rest of my life with no idea of what's to come.

EPILOGUE

A COUPLE OF MONTHS LATER

"**M**y father is coming to visit tomorrow," Alaric says. "It's the first time since everything..." he trails off, unable to finish the thought.

Not that it matters, I know exactly what he's going to say. I reach out and place my hand over his, giving it a small squeeze that I hope is reassuring.

"How is he holding up?"

"It's hard to tell from letters. I think he's all right, but he thought Mother loved him, and is now facing the fact that she probably didn't. And that his children may have inherited her powers."

I raise an eyebrow. "Do you think that?"

The crackle of the fire punctuates the silence as he thinks about my question. I smooth my hand over the blanket we've laid on the floor so we can take advantage of the warmth while being closer together than the chairs allow. Technically, he isn't supposed to be in my room at all, but it's one of those things that the staff do absolutely nothing to enforce. We're just taking advantage of that.

"No, I don't think so. I looked up some exercises in the library and tried them, but I didn't feel anything," he admits.

"But you've tried?"

Alaric chuckles. "Wouldn't you if you found out you might be magic?"

I join his laughter. "That's fair. But maybe it's because you don't have a proper teacher? We could find someone..."

"I'm fine without learning it."

"You might not have a choice. If you have it, then you need to learn how to control it," I point out. "Accidents happen when things are left to go out of control."

"I promise I'll figure it out properly. But right now, I want to focus on making sure you're all right."

"I'm fine. It's been a couple of months. Even my hands have healed." I hold them out so he can see.

He captures one of my wrists in his hands and kisses my palm gently, sending a slight shiver through me. "So long as that keeps being the case."

"I'll tell you the moment it isn't." And that's the best I can do. "But I can tell you what would make me feel even better than I already do?"

"Hmm?"

"A kiss."

Alaric lets out a small laugh. "I'm sure that can be arranged." He shuffles closer to me.

He reaches out and cups my cheek in his hand. He leans in and my eyes flutter closed, waiting for the moment our lips brush against one another.

This is the true magic in the world. The connection between us makes me feel like anything is possible. Mostly because Alaric makes me feel as if *I'm* capable of anything.

My thoughts flee as he kisses me and the only thing I'm sure of is that I'm doing a good job of living in the here and now. And I'm going to continue making the most of it at every turn.

***

Thank you for reading *Princess Of Feathers*, I hope you enjoyed it! The series continues with *Princess Of Peas*, Cordelia's story and a retelling of the Princess and the Pea.

Author Note

Thank you for reading *Princess Of Feathers*, I hope you enjoyed it!

I've wanted to do a retelling of the story I know as the Six Swans for a while now, but on researching, I found several other versions of the original story. While most of them share the same basic story, they do vary a little in the details. In the end, I think this one took most of its inspiration from the Hans Christian Andersen version (The Wild Swans) - including Elisa's name. (If you've read other books in the Grimm Academy overarching series, you may have noticed that I do try to use the names from the originals where possible). However, I did down the number of brothers to three after finding a version with that many as it was more manageable for plotting.

Both Astrid and Cordelia have stories of their own in *Princess Of Petals* and *Princess Of Scales* - Cordelia's sister, Mati, also has a book (*Song of Seas*). And if you want to head right back to the beginning of the Grimm Academy world, you can with *Spindles and Spells*, a retelling of Sleeping Beauty.

Or, if the competition aspect of this series is what you particularly enjoyed, why not hop over to *Braided Silver*, a retelling of Rapunzel set in my Untold Tales world and following Cosette as she joins a competition, escapes her tower, and finds herself a kitsune familiar!

If you want to keep up to date with new releases and other news, you can join my Facebook Reader Group or mailing list.

Stay safe & happy reading!

- Laura

Also By Laura Greenwood

Signed Paperback & Merchandise:

You can find signed paperbacks, hardcovers, and merchandise based on my series (including stickers, magnets, face masks, and more!) via my website.

Series List:

* denotes a completed series

The Obscure World

A paranormal & urban fantasy world where supernaturals live out in the open alongside humans. Each series can be read on its own, but there are cameos from past characters and mentions of previous events.

<u>Cauldron Coffee Shop</u> - <u>Broomstick Bakery</u> - <u>Obscure Academy</u> - <u>The Shifter Season</u> - <u>Grimalkin Academy</u>* - <u>City Of Blood</u>* - <u>Grimalkin Vampires</u>* - <u>Supernatural Retrieval Agency</u>* - <u>The Black Fan</u>* - <u>Sabre Woods Academy</u>* - <u>Scythe Grove Academy</u>* – <u>Ashryn Barker</u>*

The Forgotten Gods World

A fantasy romance world based on Egyptian mythology.

<u>Forgotten God</u>

The Egyptian Empire

A modern fantasy world set in an alternative timeline where the Egyptian Empire never fell.

The Apprentice Of Anubis

The Paranormal Council Universe

A paranormal romance & urban fantasy world where paranormals are hidden away from the human world, and are in search of their fated mates. Each series can be read on its own, but there are cameos from past characters and mentions of previous events.

The Paranormal Council Series* - The Fae of the Paranormal Council Universe* - Paranormal Criminal Investigations* - The Necromancer Council*

Other Series

Purple Oasis (with Arizona Tape) - Grimm Academy - Beyond The Curse* - Untold Tales* - The Dragon Duels* - Speed Dating With The

<u>Denizens Of The Underworld</u> (shared world) - <u>Seven Wardens</u>* (with Skye MacKinnon) - <u>Tales Of Clan Robbins</u> (co-written with L.A. Boruff) - <u>Firehouse Witches</u>* (with Lacey Carter Andersen & L.A. Boruff) - <u>Mountain Shifters</u>* (with Lainie Anderson)

Twin Souls Universe

A paranormal romance & urban fantasy world co-written with Arizona Tape. Each series can be read on its own, but there are cameos from past characters and mentions of previous events.

<u>Amethyst's Wand Shop Mysteries</u> - <u>Twin Souls</u>* - <u>The Vampire Detective</u>*

About Laura Greenwood

Laura is a USA Today Bestselling Author of paranormal, fantasy, urban fantasy, and contemporary romance. When she's not writing, she drinks a lot of tea, tries to resist French macarons, and works towards a diploma in Egyptology. She lives in the UK, where most of her books are set. Laura specialises in quick reads, whether you're looking for a swoonworthy romance for the bath, or an action-packed adventure for your latest journey, you'll find the perfect match amongst her books!

Follow Laura Greenwood

Website: www.authorlauragreenwood.co.uk

Mailing List: https://www.authorlauragreenwood.co.uk/p/book-sign-up.html

Facebook Group: http://facebook.com/groups/theparanormalcouncil

Facebook Page: http://facebook.com/authorlauragreenwood

Bookbub: www.bookbub.com/authors/laura-greenwood